The Legend of Food Mountain
La montaña del alimento

Adapted by / Adaptado por Harriet Rohmer

Illustrated by / Ilustrado por Graciela Carrillo

Translated into Spanish by / Traducido al español por
Alma Flor Ada & Rosalma Zubizarreta

CHILDREN'S BOOK PRESS ~ SAN FRANCISCO, CALIFORNIA

Al comienzo de nuestro mundo, el gran Dios, Quetzalcoatl,
creó a la gente de la tierra de los huesos de los antepasad

Pero la gente no tenía nada que comer
y tenían hambre.

—¡Danos comida!— gritaban.   —¡Danos comida!

In the beginning of our world, the great God, Quetzalcoatl,*
created the people of earth from the bones of the ancestors.

But there was nothing for the people to eat
and they were hungry.

"Give us food!" they cried.   "Give us food!"

*Ket -ZAL-Kwatl

3

El gran Dios, Quetzalcoatl, Rey del Cielo Occidental,
   no sabía qué darles de comer a la gente de la tierra.

El le preguntó a los otros Dioses y Diosas:
—¿Qué les daremos de comer a los niños?
—¿Qué les daremos de comer?

Pero los otros Dioses y Diosas tampoco sabían.

The great God, Quetzalcoatl, King of the Western Heaven, did not know what to feed the people of earth.

He asked the other Gods and Goddesses:
"What shall we feed the children?"
"What shall we give them to eat?"

But the other Gods and Goddesses did not know either.

Entonces una enorme hormiga colorada apareció paso a paso por
el Cielo Occidental. Llevaba granos de maíz
de brillantes colores en la boca.

—Eso se ve delicioso— dijo Quetzalcoatl.
—¿Dónde lo encontraste?—

Por mucho tiempo la hormiga no lo quiso decir.

Then an enormous red ant came crawling across
the Western Heaven. She was carrying kernels
of bright-colored corn in her mouth.

"That looks delicious," said Quetzalcoatl.
"Where did you find it?"

For a long time the ant would not say.

Por fin la hormiga cedió su secreto. Señaló
a la Montaña del Alimento. —¡Allí es donde encontré el maíz!

Inmediatamente Quetzalcoatl se transformó en una hormiga negr
Siguió a la hormiga colorada hasta la Montaña del Alimento.
La hormiga colorada le enseñó por donde entrar y juntos
arrastraron afuera una pila de maíz de brillantes colores.

Βut at last the ant gave up her secret. She pointed
to Food Mountain. "There is where I found the corn!"

Immediately, Quetzalcoatl changed himself into a black ant.
He followed the red ant to Food Mountain.
The red ant showed him how to get inside, and together
they dragged out a pile of bright-colored corn.

9

Quetzalcoatl llevó el maíz al Cielo Occidental.
 Los Dioses y Diosas lo masticaron y decidieron que era bueno
Entonces Quetzalcoatl se lo puso en los labios
a la gente recién creada.

—¡Humm! —¡Delicioso! —¡Qué sabroso! —¡Qué rico!

Y la gente comió el maíz y se volvió maravillosamente fuerte.

Quetzalcoatl brought back the corn to the Western Heaven.
 The Gods and Goddesses chewed it and decided it was good.
Then Quetzalcoatl laid it on the lips
of the newly created people.

'Hmm!"   "Delicious!"   "Wonderful!"   "Yum!"

The people ate the corn and they became amazingly strong.

Quetzalcoatl estaba contentísimo.
—La Montaña del Alimento dará de comer
a la gente de la tierra para siempre— dijo.
—Yo la traeré al Cielo Occidental
para que podamos cuidarla.

Quetzalcoatl partió de nuevo. Amarró a la Montaña del Alimento
con fuertes cuerdas y trató de llevársela.
Pero no podía moverla. Pidió ayuda.

Quetzalcoatl was overjoyed.
"Food Mountain will feed
the people of earth forever," he said.
"I will bring it back to the Western Heaven
so we can take care of it."

Quetzalcoatl set out again. He tied up Food Mountain
with heavy cords and tried to carry it away.
But he could not move it. He called for help.

La Diosa y el Dios del Calendario
   vinieron a aconsejar a Quetzalcoatl.
Dejaron caer algunos granos de maíz
y estudiaron cuidadosamente el dibujo así formado.

— Vemos que el Dios del Rayo
debe abrir la Montaña del Alimento — dijeron.
— Lo llamaremos.

14

The Goddess and God of the Calendar
 came to advise Quetzalcoatl.
They threw down some kernels of corn
and carefully studied the picture that was made.

"We see that the Lightning God
must break open Food Mountain," they said.
"We shall call him."

El Dios del Rayo llegó, pero era evidente que le pasaba algo. Tenía manchas por todo el cuerpo.

El Dios del Rayo lanzó un rayo hacia la Montaña del Alimento. La Montaña del Alimento no se abrió. Lanzó más rayos. Al fin la Montaña del Alimento se abrió. Pero el Dios del Ra estaba tan débil que se cayó, completemente agotado.

The Lightning God arrived but something was wrong with him.
He had strange spots all over his body.

He threw a lightning bolt at Food Mountain.
Food Mountain did not open. He threw more lightning bolts.
At last Food Mountain broke open. But the Lightning God
was so weak he fell down, exhausted.

La Montaña del Alimento se había abierto.
Pero no había nadie cuidándola.

De momento aparecieron los enanos de la lluvia.
Azul, blanco, amarillo, rojo.
Vinieron de los cuatro puntos del universo
y empezaron a robarse la comida.

Food Mountain was wide open,
but no one was guarding it.

Suddenly, the rain dwarfs appeared.
Blue, white, yellow, red.
They came from the four directions of the Universe,
and they began to steal the food.

19

Los enanos de la lluvia se robaron toda la comida.
   Se lo llevaron todo.
El maíz blanco. El maíz negro. El maíz amarillo. El maíz rojo.

Los enanos de la lluvia se llevaron los frijoles y
las hierbas aromáticas.
Se robaron todos los tesoros de la Montaña del Alimento.

The rain dwarfs stole all the food.
  They took everything.
White corn. Black corn. Yellow corn. Red corn.

The rain dwarfs stole the beans and
the sweet-smelling grasses.
They stole all the treasures of Food Mountain.

Y desde entonces, la gente de la tierra
llama a las lluvias para que regresen
y les traigan alimento.

And from that time on, the people of earth
have called for the rains to come back
and bring them food.

The Legend of Food Mountain is adapted from the Chimalpopocatl Codice, one of several picture-writing manuscripts recorded by native priests after the Spanish conquest of Mexico. Many of the symbols used by Graciela Carrillo in her illustrations come directly from these old codices. The symbol for Food Mountain (the earth) looks like this:

Raindrops look like this:

Speech or song is depicted by different kinds of "bubbles":

As with any story that has survived over the centuries, this one works on many levels.
  It is a story of origins: how the present human race was created from the bones of the ancestors and how the Gods and Goddesses discovered that corn could feed the people. It is also a drama of the conflict between the civilizing God, Quetzalcoatl, and the warlike rain God, Tlaloc.

But, most important for today's children, The Legend of Food Mountain reminds us that food must be respected as a part of life. It is important to understand that everything that nourishes us has been nurtured by the earth; and in return, we must make sure that the earth is cared for. In this way, the crops will continue to grow, the people and animals will continue to eat, and the great cycle of life on this planet will survive and flourish.

Harriet Rohmer

Graciela Carrillo is a painter and muralist. Her murals depicting the power and beauty of Aztlan (Mexico and the southwest United States) can be seen on the walls of San Francisco and Oakland, California, and Santa Fe, New Mexico.

Series Editor: Harriet Rohmer
Hand Lettering: Roger I Reyes
Book Design: Harriet Rohmer, Robin Cherin, Roger I Reyes, Graciela Carrillo
Production: Robin Cherin

Library of Congress Cataloging-in-Publication Data

Rohmer, Harriet.
    The legend of food mountain.

    English and Spanish.
    Summary: An Aztec legend recounting how a giant red ant helped the ancient god, Quetzalcoatl, bring corn to the first hungry people of the earth.
    1. Aztecs—Legends. 2. Indians of Mexico—Legends. 3. Corn—Folklore—Juvenile literature. [1. Aztecs—Legends. 2. Indians of Mexico—Legends] I. Carrillo de López, Graciela, ill. II. Title III. Title: La montaña del alimento.
F1219.76.F65R6518 1988 398.2'4525796'08997 88-18946
ISBN 0-89239-022-0